This book
belongs to:
....

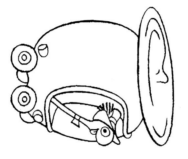

SIMON SPOTLIGHT
An imprint of Simon & Schuster Children's Publishing Division
1230 Avenue of the Americas
New York, New York 10020

Text copyright © 1998 by the Estate of Richard Scarry

Adapted from the nonfiction segments entitled "Imagine That," "How To Be Safe," and "How It Works" from the animated television series *The Busy World of Richard Scarry*™, produced by Paramount Pictures and Cinar.

All rights reserved including the right of reproduction in whole or in part in any form.

SIMON SPOTLIGHT and colophon are registered trademarks of Simon & Schuster.

Designed and produced by Les Livres du Dragon D'Or

Manufactured in Italy

First Edition   10 9 8 7 6 5 4 3 2 1

ISBN 0-689-81633-2

Lowly Worm's How, Where, & Why Books

X-Rays
and
Other Fun Things

X-Rays
Where Bread
Comes From
The Sun
On the Street

Simon Spotlight

X-RAYS

X-rays are invisible rays
that allow you to see
through things.
Isn't that amazing?
Come have a look!

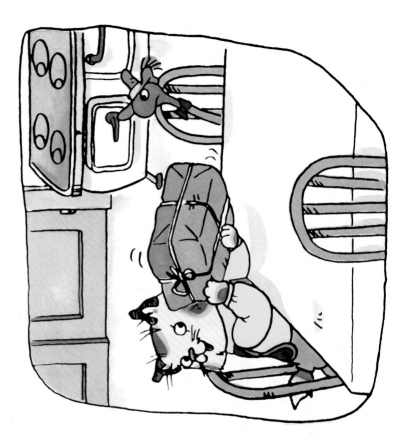

"I wonder what
is inside this
package?"
says Huckle.
"It would be great
if we had
X-ray vision!"

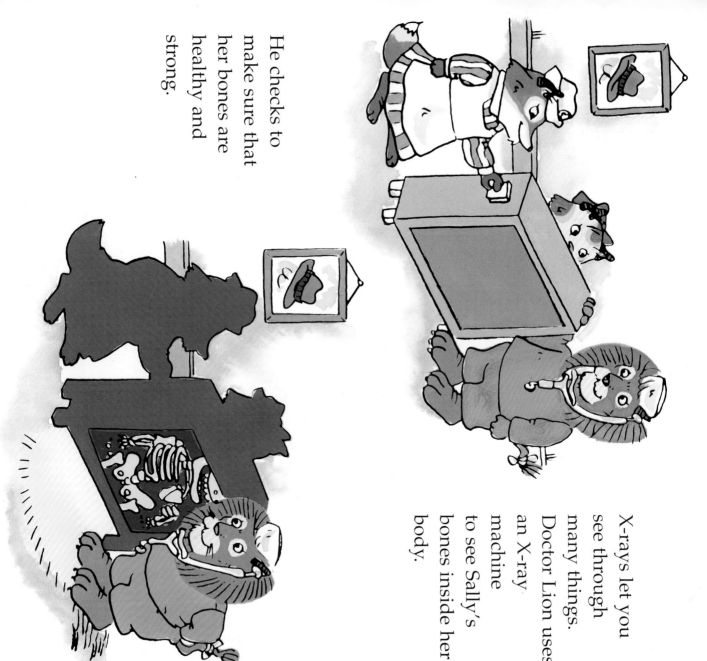

X-rays let you see through many things. Doctor Lion uses an X-ray machine to see Sally's bones inside her body.

He checks to make sure that her bones are healthy and strong.

Airports also use X-ray machines to look inside luggage.
The outlines of objects inside the luggage appear
on a special TV screen.

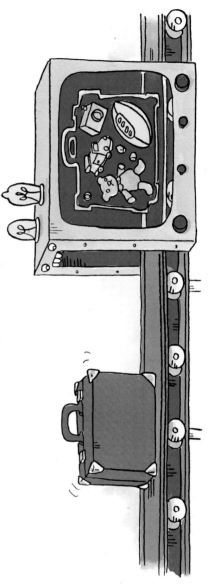

Imagine if you had X-ray vision to see inside Mr. Frumble and his pickle car.

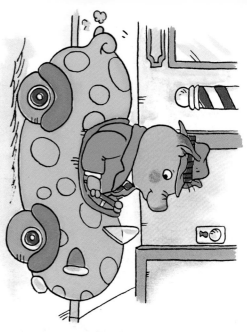

Whoa! Doesn't he look funny?

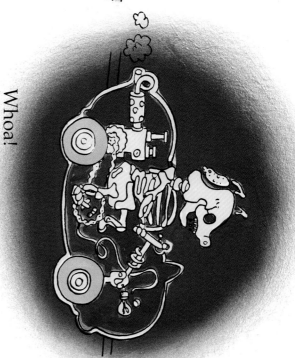

"Look! Here is what is inside the package!" Huckle shows Lowly. "It's a glass pitcher!"

"We don't need X-ray vision to see inside that!" chuckles Lowly.

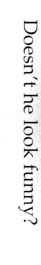

WHERE BREAD COMES FROM

Do you know where bread comes from? Let's find out!

"I made my favorite sandwich for lunch—peanut butter and jelly!" Huckle tells Lowly. "Do you want one?"

"No, thank you, Huckle," Lowly replies. "I prefer an apple sandwich. But do you know where bread comes from?"

Bread is made out of wheat. When it is time to harvest the wheat crop, farmers use a harvesting machine to separate the grain from the wheat stalks and dirt.

The grains are poured into a bag and taken to a place called the flour mill.

At the mill, the grains are put in a grinder. The grinder crushes the grains again and again until they become flour.

Then the flour is put in large bags and taken to the bakery. What a trip, so far!

At the bakery, Baker Humperdink mixes flour with water, salt, and yeast to make dough. He kneads the dough and shapes the loaves. Then into the oven they go to bake!

Once baked, the loaves
come out hot and tasty!

"These look and smell delicious,
Humperdink!" says Lowly.

"I know now where bread
comes from!" says Huckle.
"And I also know where it is
going! Yum!"

THE SUN

A sunny day can be lots of fun,
but be careful:
The sun can be dangerous
because of its hot, hot rays.
But if you protect yourself
from them, you won't have
trouble from the sun!

Pop! Pop! Pop!
"Look at that corn car, Lowly!" Huckle exclaims.

"The sun has turned it
into a popcorn car!"

"Gee! Imagine what the sun could do to us!" Huckle says.

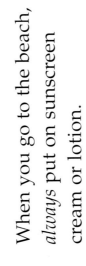

When you go to the beach, *always* put on sunscreen cream or lotion.

And don't forget your sunglasses and hat!

Try to stay in the shade between ten A.M. and three P.M. That's when the sun is the hottest!

Playing in the sun can be lots of fun!

But don't overdo it. You'll get too hot!

When it's hot, drink lots of water and try to stay in the shade.

Ahhh!

"Now I feel much better," Lowly says.

When it's hot, keeping cool is the smart thing to do!
Right, Huckle? Right, Lowly?

ON THE STREET

When you cross the street you should always be very careful. Pay attention to cars and trucks because they may not see you. Let's follow Huckle and Lowly through Busytown!

"Come on, Lowly," Huckle says. "We have to buy groceries at the market before it closes."

Vrooomm!
Look out, Huckle!
That truck could have run you over!

Always **stop**, **look** both ways . . .

and **listen!**

Then, if there is no car coming, you can cross the street.

"Hi, Hilda!"

Never cross between parked cars, because drivers can't see you at all!

Pay attention to the traffic lights and don't *ever* cross when the light is red. Right, Sergeant Murphy?

When the light is green and "Walk" appears, look around, then cross, but don't run.

Oh, no!
The grocery store is closed!
"Well, almost," says Grocer Hank, letting the boys inside.
"Thank you, Hank!" say Huckle and Lowly.

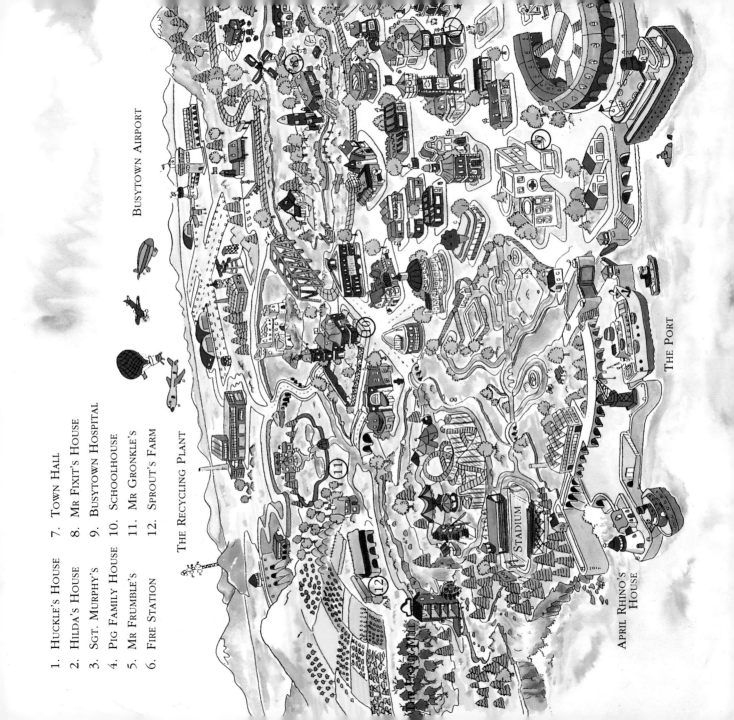

BUSYTOWN AIRPORT

THE PORT

THE RECYCLING PLANT

APRIL RHINO'S HOUSE

STADIUM

1. HUCKLE'S HOUSE
2. HILDA'S HOUSE
3. SGT. MURPHY'S
4. PIG FAMILY HOUSE
5. MR FRUMBLE'S
6. FIRE STATION
7. TOWN HALL
8. MR FIXIT'S HOUSE
9. BUSYTOWN HOSPITAL
10. SCHOOLHOUSE
11. MR GRONKLE'S
12. SPROUT'S FARM

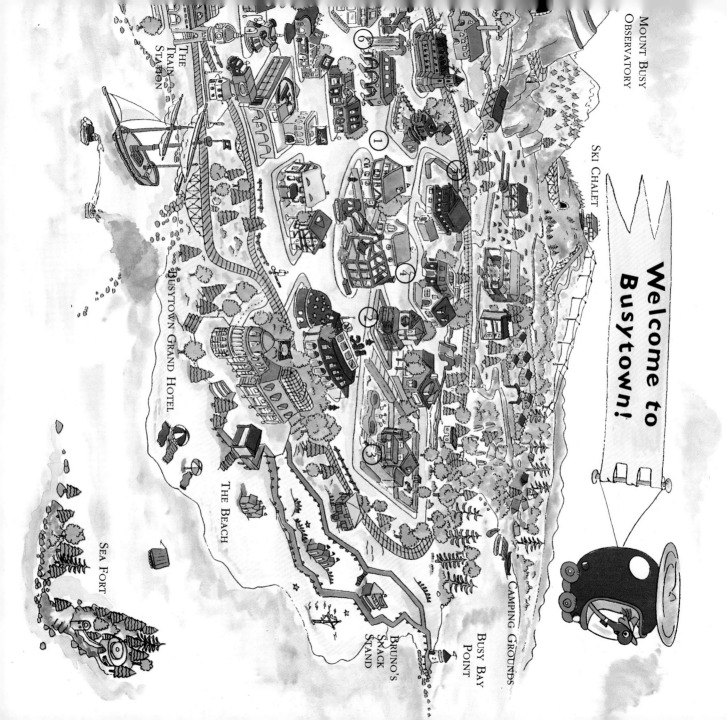

Welcome to Busytown!

MOUNT BUSY OBSERVATORY

SKI CHALET

THE TRAIN STATION

BUSYTOWN GRAND HOTEL

THE BEACH

SEA FORT

BRUNO'S SNACK STAND

BUSY BAY POINT

CAMPING GROUNDS

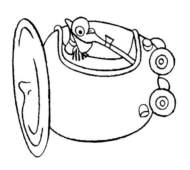